W9-BCQ-636

You Can Go Jump

Modern Curriculum Press
BEGINNING
TO
READ
Series

ISBN 0-8136-5082-8 (Hardbound)
ISBN 0-8136-5582-X (Paperback)

7 8 9 10   99

You Can Go Jump

Valjean McLenighan

illustrated by Jared D. Lee

MODERN CURRICULUM PRESS
CLEVELAND · TORONTO

7

8

9

At the big house.

17

Jump. Jump.

There! Take that, you thing, you.

23

25

27

Valjean McLenighan is a writer, editor, and producer.

Word List: All of the 94 words used in *You Can Go Jump* are listed. Regular plurals and verb forms of words already on the list are not listed separately, but the endings are given in parentheses after the word.

1	you		ball		am		in
	can		will		long	**20**	again
	go(ing)		give	**12**	stop	**21**	him
	jump(er)		me	**13**	at	**23**	that
4	what	**7**	want		the		thing
	see		have		big	**24**	later
	is		this		house		guess
	get		thank(s)		father	**26**	where
	oh		but		little		it
	yes	**8**	not		one		began
	no		be		eat		last
	help(ed)		funny	**14**	she		birthday
5	hello	**9**	to		away		was
	there		take	**15**	did		play(ing)
	good		home		a		new
	look(ing, s)		with		day		toys
	come		your(s)		too		then
	on		pet		bad		heard
6	so		say	**16**	knock		something
	I		he		who		door
	do	**10**	and		soon	**28**	surprise(d)
	for	**11**	here		out	**29**	year
	find		are	**18**	said		
	my		now	**19**	like		